W9-BIA-920

The Seagoing Cowboy

By Peggy Reiff Miller
Illustrated by Claire Ewart

Brethren Press

*To Alten and Isaac, in honor of your Great-great-grandpa
Abraham Theodore Reiff, our family's own seagoing cowboy;
and to all the seagoing cowboys who have so graciously
shared your stories with me—you're a blessing.*

—P.R.M.

*For Stanley, Robert, and Caryl, who loved the wind and
the waves. Sail on, sailors.*

—C.E.

The Seagoing Cowboy
Text © 2016 Peggy Reiff Miller
Illustrations © 2016 Claire Ewart

BRETHREN PRESS is registered in the U.S. Patent and Trademark Office by
the Church of the Brethren, 1451 Dundee Avenue, Elgin, Illinois 60120.

For information about permission to reproduce selections from this book,
visit www.brethrenpress.com or write to Brethren Press, Attn: Permissions,
1451 Dundee Avenue, Elgin, Illinois 60120.

Library of Congress Cataloging-in-Publication Data

Miller, Peggy Reiff, 1947-
  The seagoing cowboy / written by Peggy Reiff Miller ; illustrated by Claire Ewart.
    pages cm
  Summary: "A young man seeks adventure as a 'seagoing cowboy' taking care of
heifers on a ship to Poland after World War II and finds much more"—Provided by publisher.
  ISBN 978-0-87178-212-0 (hardcover)
  [1. Cowboys—Fiction. 2. Ships—Fiction. 3. World War, 1939-1945—Fiction.] I. Ewart, Claire, illustrator. II. Title.
  PZ7.1.M586Se 2016
  [E]—dc23
                                                                2015013613

20 19 18 17 16   1 2 3 4 5

Printed in the United States of America

A long time ago,
when I was looking for adventure,
I became a "seagoing cowboy."

Seagoing cowboys didn't ride horses.
We rode waves.
Seagoing cowboys didn't herd cattle across prairies.
We herded them across the ocean.
We took farm animals to people who had been in a terrible war.

It was a long, but exciting, journey.
My friend John went with me.
We rode the train to the city
where our ship was waiting for us.

WOODSTOCK VICT

The port was a noisy, busy place:
Dock workers and seamen hustled and bustled.
Boat whistles blew.
Cranes cranked.
Horses neighed and heifers bawled
as they were lifted onto the ship in their "flying stalls."

Before we could sail, all of us "cowboys" had to get four shots.
That hurt!
But now I knew I wouldn't get sick with smallpox,
tetanus, typhus, or typhoid fever.

Then our crew leader came and took us on board.
When we stepped on deck, John got a big surprise.
There was his family's work horse Queenie, whinnying at him!

Before our trip, John's father had
sold Queenie to buy a tractor.
And here she was, waiting to go
to Poland, just like us.

Our ship soon pulled out to sea.
It rocked gently on the water,
up and down
and all around.

And those shots we got?

They didn't keep me
from getting seasick!

But sick or not,
we cowboys
had work to do.

John got to take care of Queenie and other horses.
I took care of heifers.

One of my heifers was named Hope.
She was sent by boys and girls from a church in Pennsylvania.
One day, Hope had a surprise for us . . .

. . . a calf we named Joy.

Another day, we ran into a bad storm.
"Stay in your cabin," the captain ordered,
"so the waves don't toss you into the ocean."

Instead, the waves tossed us
in our bunks.

When the storm was over,
I hurried to see if Hope and her calf were all right.
John ran to check on Queenie.
All of the animals were safe.

For ten long days there was
nothing to see but ocean.

Then, we spotted land.
"Hooray!" we shouted.

But we still had another week to travel.
Up the English Channel we went,
through the Kiel Canal,
across the Baltic Sea.
Finally, our ship docked in the country of Poland.

24

Two boys played music to welcome us.
Dock workers got busy unloading our animals.
We cowboys went on shore to explore.

Children followed us everywhere.
They wanted gum—goomi, they called it—and chocolate.
People were happy to see us and our horses and heifers.
But what we saw in Poland made us sad.

The war had left the country in ruins.
Many people had nothing left.
They had lost their homes.
They had lost people they loved.
They had lost the animals
that plowed their fields and gave them food.
Our horses and heifers would give them a new start.

Queenie and other horses went to a large barn in the country. Polish farmers came to the barn to get their new work horses. Now they would be able to plow their fields again.

Hope and her calf went to an orphanage.
The children who lived there had little to eat because of the war.
Now they would have milk and butter and cheese.

The children sang for us and didn't want us to leave.
But we had to return to the ship.
After five days in Poland, the captain was ready to take us home.

As we pulled away from the shores of Poland,
I waved goodbye to the people there.
I knew I would never forget them.
I would also never forget the terrible things that war can do.

I had started out looking
for an adventure,
but I found so much more.
I'm glad I was a seagoing cowboy.

Ships and trips

Jack M. Clouse

Unpredictable weather
Sometimes winter storms caused ships to stay in Europe until the ice thawed.

Roy Auernheimer

The *S.S. Woodstock Victory* was one of more than 70 ships used to deliver livestock. The *Woodstock Victory* made five trips to Poland in 1946.

Smelly work
Seagoing cowboys had to pull up buckets of manure to be thrown overboard.

Ernest Bechman

Newport News, Virginia

Wayne Zook

Mess hall
Cowboys had their own dining room separate from the ship's crew. Sometimes dishes would slide off the table onto the floor.

Jacob C. Wine, Jr.

All aboard Ships like the *Woodstock Victory* held close to 800 animals and required about 32 seagoing cowboys.

Eugene K. Souder

Across the ocean When the men saw the White Cliffs of Dover and the bridges over the Kiel Canal, they knew they were almost there.

Paul Kanagy

Charles B. Shenk

Kiel Canal

Dover

Gdansk

POLAND

Cost of war When the cowboys arrived on shore, they saw a city in ruins.

Ivan Meck

Joseph M. Long

Laundry day
Cowboys had to do their laundry, however they could. Some tied their clothes to a rope and dragged them behind the ship.

Roger Ingold

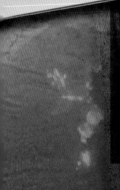

Elmer J. Bowers

Sleeping quarters
Cowboys usually slept at the back of the ship, where they felt the up-and-down motion of the ship more than the crew did.

37

Author's note

My Grandpa Abe was a "seagoing cowboy," but I never heard his story. After he died, my father gave me some photos from Grandpa's trip. The pictures made me curious. What was it like to be a seagoing cowboy? So I started asking men I knew who had made the trips.

No one trip happened exactly like the story in this book, but every event in the story is true as documented in my interviews with these seagoing cowboys and in their diaries and photos—including the event of 18-year-old John Nunemaker of Goshen, Indiana, finding his horse Queenie on his ship.

The seagoing cowboys were a group of about 7,000 men, ages 16 to 72, who signed up to take care of livestock sent to Europe and China after World War II. The animals were shipped by the United Nations Relief and Rehabilitation Administration (UNRRA) and Heifer Project.

Forty-four nations, united in their efforts during the war, created UNRRA in 1943 to provide help to countries hurt by the fighting. Earlier that year, the Brethren Service Committee of the Church of the Brethren approved a plan proposed by church leader Dan West to send pregnant heifers overseas to help people in need. This plan, already in place in Dan's Northern Indiana District of the Church of the Brethren, was the Heifer Project.

In 1945, at the close of World War II, UNRRA agreed to ship Heifer Project's animals free of charge. In return, the Brethren Service Committee agreed to recruit all of the cattle attendants UNRRA needed for their 360 livestock shipments: The seagoing cowboy program was born.

The seagoing cowboys came from all over the United States and Canada and from all walks of life. They were farmers and students, teachers and preachers, bankers and carpenters. They came from many different religions and races. After witnessing the wounds of war, many of them dedicated their lives to working for peace and

Virginian Cattle Crew in Poland

many entered service professions such as pastoral ministry or social work.

UNRRA and Heifer Project shipped livestock to Albania, Belgium, China, Ethiopia, France, Greece, Italy, and Poland. Shipments also went to Czechoslovakia, via ports in Germany, and to Yugoslavia via Trieste, Italy. Horses, heifers, and mules were the main livestock shipped, but many chicks and some sheep, pigs, and goats were also sent. To learn more about this little-known history, go to www.seagoingcowboys.com.

UNRRA lasted only about two years after World War II ended. Heifer Project, however, continued. For over four decades, Heifer Project's seagoing, airgoing, and land cowboys and cowgirls helped to transport animals to countries all over the world, starting with countries like Japan and Germany

Hope on Christmas Day at the Villa Skaut orphanage in Konstancin.

which had been our enemies during the war. Heifer Project grew into today's independent, award-winning development organization called Heifer International. Today, Heifer International buys animals from the regions close to where they are needed to save on shipping costs and to obtain animals better adapted to local climates and diseases. To learn more about Heifer International, go to www.heifer.org.

Although the Brethren Service Committee no longer exists, the Church of the Brethren continues to be a service-oriented denomination. It is one of the three Historic Peace Churches, along with the Quakers (Religious Society of Friends) and the Mennonites. To learn more about the Church of the Brethren, go to www.brethren.org.

—*Peggy Reiff Miller*